This Book Belongs

MW00824057

Mrs. Raitt

Still I Fly

NIKKI ACE

ILLUSTRATED BY: Wesley Ace Jr. and Dani Ace

Mrs. Raitt

Everyone calls me Victor.

I'm a *tenacious* lil' fly -

full of adventures every morning
till the sun sets in the sky.

When I wake
my tummy *growls*,
telling me,
"I'm hungry now!"
So I start to search and search
to find food
and quench my thirst.

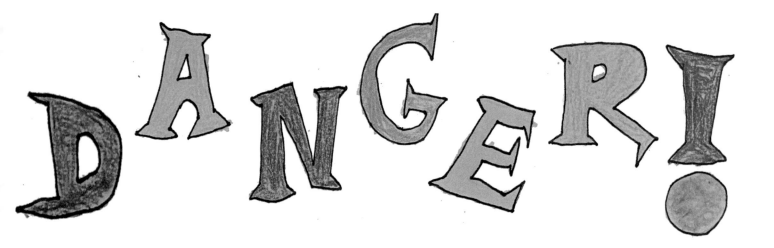

DANGER!

Without a doubt,
danger lurks,
surprising me
like *fireworks!*
Hurdles I'll jump,
but I'll survive.
By nightfall . . .

... still I fly.

I like going to this house
because he lets his food *decay*:
Trash cans filled with food that's rot,
spoiled fruit in a fruit tray.
But there's always a challenge
that seems to get in the way
of me getting my grub on,
Oh! Oh! . . . I've been seen – MUST FLY AWAY!

Now I'm in hot water,
but I won't go **BERSERK,**
even if the fly swatter
tries to swat me off planet earth . . .
being swung like a baseball bat
- so hard -
I'd be buried in dirt.
But with a *swing* and a *miss*
I fled with no scratch and unhurt.

I *swished* and **slammed**

and *dipped* and *pranced*,
did a flip, arms up
like a gymnast when I land.
And I finished my victory
with a quick special dance.
Going to this home was risky -
surely taking a chance.

But I just had to go!
My tummy is *rumbling* – No lie!
It's a risk I had to take
and as you see . . .

... still I fly.

I'm still not satisfied.
Still hunger is my struggle.
I'll take my chances in the wild
with all this food in the jungle.
But with no hesitation,
I'm seen as food from wasp.
He tries to block my destination,

so I pull out my *boxing gloves*.

2 upper cuts to the body.
3 jabs to the face.
Right hooks and left hooks -
wasp got *punched* all over the place.

He learned really quickly,
he messed with the wrong fly,
so wasp started fleeing and . . .

. . . still I fly.

Next thing I know,
I see happy *frog* on a lily pad
just chillin' and relaxin',
then her happy went to bad!

It was like slow motion
as it came towards me . . .
her *tongue* in locomotion
with absolutely no warning.

With a **zoom** and a **"Buzzzzz!"**
and a **bash** and a **zip**,
I escaped the frog's tongue,
then showed off with a **skip**.
Did not want to get stuck
in her thick honey-like spit
or get wrapped like a burrito
as her tongue folds and twists.

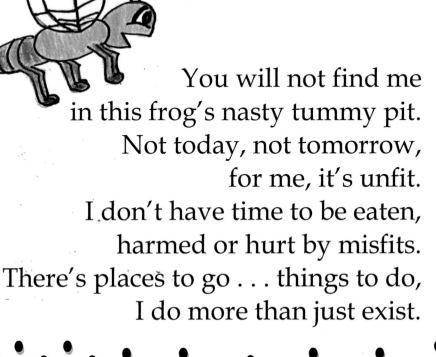

You will not find me
in this frog's nasty tummy pit.
Not today, not tomorrow,
for me, it's unfit.
I don't have time to be eaten,
harmed or hurt by misfits.
There's places to go . . . things to do,
I do more than just exist.

Frog was *baffled* and confused.
My moves were just so sly,
since I got away uneaten and . . .

. . . still I fly.

From afar, I could see
a beautiful sight calling my name.
It said, *"Victor come to me
and eat what I proudly create."*

As I flew towards this sight
my eyes must have gone blind.

I didn't see spider's web
built to catch so spider can dine.

I faintly heard words of caution
saying, *"BUZZ, BUZZ, BUZZ !"*
as onlooking friends and family
warn, **"A *trap!*"** out of love.
So I make a quick right
to not get caught in spider's web
and thought how grateful that I am
having great *seeing* family and friends.

I look back and give a wave,
"Good looking out!"
I shout my praise.
And with a "thanks" and a "goodbye"
I'm so amazed that . . .

. . . still I fly.

My antennae are detectives.
They will notice any odor.

I smell yummy *nectar* goodness
coming from way down yonder.
As I get closer and closer,
my view gets even more alluring
when I see the plant called Venus
oozing nectar . . .
I start soaring!

Venus calls my name again
offering nectar on her leaves,
but as soon as my eating begins
she snaps shut . . . trapping me.
I squeezed through her PRISON BARS,
since I'm a clever little guy,
singing joyfully to the blue sky,
I'm taking flight and . . .

... still I fly.

So, no matter what *adventure*

or obstacle I face,
when a swatter swats at me
all over the place,
or if I get in a boxing match
with wasp trying to eat,
or if frog's tongue tries to snatch

my life to eat as meat,

or when spider makes a web
that friends and family help me see,
or how Venus the fly trap
attracts me with trickery . . .
I live my life true to my name.
They don't call me Victor for nothing.

Victorious is who I became

when others want me for hunting.

At last, I found some grub
that a doggy left behind.
Now I can regain my strength
for tomorrow's adventures by and by.
I'm prepared for what's ahead.
It's just the way I was designed.

Funny how I can even land in *poop* and . . .

. . . still I fly.

AUTHOR
(Also colored most illustrations)

Nikki Ace

I do not like flies. No I don't!
I'll never like flies. No I won't!
They're pests and annoying,
buzzing in my ear,
landing on my food . . .
Why don't they just disappear?

This uninvited guest
just flying in my house,
but one day
a determined fly
for some reason just stood out.

No matter how many swings
from my hands or the swatter,
could block this lil' fly
from fulfilling his hunger.

He just kept on living,
so I let the fly be.
He flew fast and was clever
and he taught me one thing.
He fought for his precious life,
so he received respect from me.
Instead of destroying this fly,
I opened my door to let him flee.

I learned, no matter how worthless
others think you are,
my life is full of **God's purpose**,
and *still I fly* is my call.

. . . .

Nikki Ace lives in Los Angeles, California with her lovely husband
of 12 years – Wesley Ace – and her two amazing children –
Wesley Ace Jr. and Dani Ace. She has authored *ten books* with the
expectation of helping people understand the *beauty of God* and
how He created each and every one of us in His incredible image.

ILLUSTRATORS

Wesley Ace Jr.
10 years old- Head Illustrator

Wesley's interests include baseball, playing the guitar, reading – history, realistic fiction, fantasy books - and making people laugh with his wit and charm.

Dani Ace
5 years old – Assistant Illustrator

Dani is fascinated by the beauty of horses, relishes in reading "girlie" books, and is extremely passionate about her singing and dancing.

This book is dedicated to every single person –big or small - that reads this book. You are all VICTORS because you were born to be a WINNER!

To my best friend, my love, and my life partner - Wesley Ace - thank you for giving me the opportunity to fulfill what I believe God has purposed me to do. You have helped me to continue to reach toward my God-given potential and there is no one that I would rather flourish in life with. Incredible father and husband is an understatement – I'll simply call you a WINNER!
~With love always, Nikki

"We are more than
CONQUERORS
through Christ who loved us."
-Romans 8:37-

Made in the USA
San Bernardino, CA
09 July 2019